WELCOME TO

Collect the special coins in this book.
You will earn one gold coin for
every chapter you read.

Once you have finished all the chapters,
find out what to do with your gold coins at
the back of the book.

With special thanks to Cherith Baldry

To James Noble –

the boy who would be Tom

www.beastquest.co.uk

ORCHARD BOOKS
Carmelite House
50 Victoria Embankment
London EC4Y 0DZ

A Paperback Original
First published in Great Britain in 2007
This edition published in 2015

Beast Quest is a registered trademark of Beast Quest Limited
Series created by Beast Quest Limited, London

Text © Beast Quest Limited 2007
Cover illustration © David Wyatt 2007
Inside illustrations © Beast Quest Limited 2007

A CIP catalogue record for this book is available from
the British Library.

ISBN 978 1 40834 764 5

1

Printed and bound by CPI Group (UK) Ltd, Croydon, CR0 4YY

MIX
Paper from
responsible sources
FSC® C104740

The paper and board used in this book are made from wood
from responsible sources.

Orchard Books
An imprint of Hachette Children's Group
Part of The Watts Publishing Group Limited
An Hachette UK Company

www.hachette.co.uk

SeproN
THE SEA SERPENT

BY ADAM BLADE

ORCHARD

THE IC[Y]

THE NORTHERN
MOUNTAINS

WESTERN OCEAN

THE FOREST
OF FEAR

CONTENTS

Welcome to the Kingdom of Avantia. I am Aduro – a Good Wizard residing in the palace of King Hugo. You join us at a difficult time. Let me explain...

The Ancient Scripts say that our peaceful kingdom shall one day be plunged into peril.

Now that time has come.

Under the evil spell of Malvel the Dark Wizard, six Beasts – fire dragon, sea serpent, mountain giant, horse-man, snow monster and flame bird – run wild and destroy the land they once protected.

Avantia is in danger, but the Ancient Scripts also predict an unlikely hero. It is written that a boy shall take up the Quest to free the Beasts from the curse and save the kingdom.

We do not know who this boy is, only that his time has come...

We pray our young hero will have the courage and the heart to take up the Quest. Will you join us as we wait and watch?

Avantia salutes you,

Aduro

PROLOGUE

The fishing boat rocked gently on the waves. Calum loosened the rope and let down the sail. His father began to cast out the net, hissing softly through his teeth as he worked.

"I don't know why we bother," he grumbled. "We haven't caught anything for a month!"

"You know what they say," Calum

said. "The sea serpent has scared away the fish."

His father snorted. "Old wives' tales! Anyway, I thought that sea serpent was meant to help us."

Calum glanced round, shivering slightly. Nothing broke the surface of the sea except for a small rocky island not far from the beach.

When they hauled in the net, there was nothing in it.

"Useless," his father said.

He cast the net out again. As Calum watched it sink into the depths of the water, he spotted something happening between the boat and the shore. It looked as if the sea was boiling. Then it began to churn angrily, and foam and waves dashed against the rocks.

"Look!" he cried, pointing. "Over there!"

His father turned, grabbing the side of the boat as it started to rock dangerously.

Then, out of the water rose a

monstrous head on a long, slender neck. It was covered in thick, rainbow-coloured scales and barnacles. A golden collar round the Beast's neck glinted in the sunshine, and a glowing chain stretched from this down into the water.

"What is it?" Calum's father yelled.

Calum scrambled for the rope to raise the sail, but it was too late. The Beast's neck arched and its vast head loomed over the boat. Calum stared up into huge, furious eyes that seemed to burn with cold fire. Choking with terror, he saw the creature's jaws gape open. Its long, curving fangs snapped the boat's mast, and splinters showered down on father and son like rain.

Sea water slopped over Calum

as the boat tilted. Cowering down,
he wrapped his arms over his head
and squeezed his eyes shut, as the

roar of the sea serpent echoed all
around him...

THE ROAD TO THE WEST

Tom brought Storm to a halt at the foot of a rocky slope. He and Elenna slid to the ground so that the horse could rest. Silver the wolf flopped down beside them, his tongue lolling out as he panted.

The hill where Tom had met and battled Ferno the Fire Dragon was far behind them. Now he and

Elenna were heading west on the next stage of their Beast Quest.

Tom's heart began thumping again as he remembered how he had freed Ferno from the curse of Malvel the Dark Wizard. The dragon had burnt crops all over Avantia and blocked the river, making the land dry and barren. When Tom had unlocked the magic collar that imprisoned him, the dragon was released from the spell. As he flew away, he had dislodged the stones damming the river, and a foaming torrent had gushed down the hillside.

"I'll never forget how Ferno broke the rocks with his tail," Elenna said, as if she guessed what Tom was thinking. "Or how you leapt up on his wing! That was really brave."

"It wouldn't have worked if you hadn't shot that arrow up to me, with the key tied to it," Tom replied, feeling embarrassed by Elenna's praise. "I'd never have unlocked the collar without that."

"What you did was still the bravest thing I've ever seen," Elenna insisted.

"We both freed Ferno," Tom said firmly. "And now Avantia has water again."

"Yes, and no more burnt crops," Elenna agreed.

Silver leapt up again with an impatient yelp.

Elenna turned to Tom, a

determined look in her eyes. "We'd better push on," she said.

Tom could still hear the words of Wizard Aduro ringing in his ears. Freeing Ferno the Fire Dragon was only the first of his tasks. Malvel's curse had turned the Good Beasts of Avantia into evil monsters that were destroying the kingdom. It was Tom's Quest to free all the Beasts and save his people. Tom wasn't sure he could succeed. There was so much he had to do and so many Beasts to conquer! But he meant to try, with all the strength and courage he had.

While there's blood in my veins, he thought, *I will not give up.*

This was the adventure Tom had

been waiting for all his life. And even though his father, Taladon the Swift, had disappeared when Tom was a baby, he was determined to make him proud.

"Let's have another look at the map," he said.

He pulled out the scroll that Wizard Aduro had given him. On it a path glowed green, winding through hills and woodland until it reached the sea in the west.

As Tom looked at the map, a tiny head reared out of the waves drawn on the paper, just beside a spike of rock that looked like an island. A jagged tail slapped down, sending spray high into the air. Tom started as a drop splashed onto his hand.

"There's Sepron," said Elenna.
Her voice was filled with awe.

"I still can't believe it!" said Tom.
"A sea serpent!"

"He's angry." Elenna's eyes were
wide, as if she had just realised the
huge mission facing them. "How do
you think he is destroying Avantia?"

"I don't know," Tom said, then he

added boldly, "But whatever he's doing, we're going to stop it. That's part of our Quest."

Silver let out another loud yelp. He grabbed the corner of Elenna's cloak in his teeth and tugged gently. At the foot of the slope, Storm scraped one hoof impatiently on the stones.

Tom laughed. "All right, I know. It's time we were going."

He checked the map one last time and stowed it away in his pocket. Before he scrambled back onto Storm, he made sure that the shield Wizard Aduro had given him was firmly strapped to his back. It had been scorched by Ferno, but one of the dragon's bluish-black scales shone in its slot on the shield's surface. Was it true, Tom wondered, that the shield could now protect them from fire?

He swung himself into the saddle. Elenna sprang up behind him and wrapped her arms round his waist. Tom patted Storm's glossy black neck.

"On to the west!" he cried.

At first the path zigzagged up the slope, then through a belt of trees. By the time the sun went down they had reached a pass that curved through a range of low hills.

Tom stopped beside a pool and slid to the ground. "This would be a good place to make camp."

Elenna helped him to unsaddle Storm so the horse could drink from the pool. Silver stood beside him, lapping thirstily. Tom scooped a handful of cool water into his mouth then started to collect sticks for a fire.

"I'm starving!" said Elenna. "I'll see if there are any nuts or berries on these bushes."

While she was searching, Storm cropped the grass beside the path.

"We've nothing for Silver to eat," said Tom.

"He'll find something for himself," Elenna replied. "Go on, boy." She patted the wolf and shooed him away.

Silver waved his tail and vanished among the rocks. He returned before Tom and Elenna had finished eating, and they all settled down for the night.

Tom looked up at the stars, thinking about Sepron. He hoped they could reach the coast soon, before the Beast had the chance to harm the kingdom further.

They set off again early the next morning, and soon reached the edge of the hills. A long, smooth slope was in front of them. Far ahead Tom could make out the distant glimmer of the sea and a tiny rocky island.

"We're almost there!" Elenna exclaimed.

A flash of light on the water caught Tom's eye. He gasped.

"What's the matter?" Elenna asked.

"I'm not sure...but I think I saw Sepron."

He felt Elenna's grip on him tighten. "Where?"

"Over there, near that island." Tom pointed. "But he's gone now."

He dug his heels into Storm's side to urge him on. Soon the path levelled and they rode through farmland. Everything seemed deserted. Great patches of ground were covered in burnt stubble.

"Look!" Elenna pointed to the blackened timbers of what had been a farmhouse. "Ferno was here."

A shiver ran through Tom, even though he knew the dragon was now free from Malvel's evil spell and would never blast the land with fire again. He urged Storm to a faster trot, eager to keep moving. Silver bounded a few paces ahead.

Suddenly, Storm reared. His forelegs pawed the air.

Elenna squealed in alarm and gripped Tom to stop herself sliding off.

"Storm – steady!" Tom yelled.

When the horse's forelegs fell to the ground he began skittering to one side. Tom tugged on the reins but couldn't get him under control. Then he noticed that Silver was standing still, his legs stiff and the bushy grey fur on his shoulders bristling. He began whining uneasily.

"Something's wrong," said Elenna. "Silver always knows."

Tom glanced back at Elenna, noticing the alarm in her eyes. He looked round but saw nothing, just empty fields. There was no sign of danger. But Silver was still whimpering and Storm was tossing his head, his eyes rolling in panic. Beads of sweat had broken out on his black coat.

"What is it, boy?" Tom was still struggling to keep the terrified horse on the path. "What's the matter?"

Silver let out a howl. He was staring straight ahead. Following

his gaze, Tom thought he could
make out something moving on the
horizon. A silver line had appeared,
stretching as far as he could see in
both directions. Sunlight glinted on
it and then Tom could see watery
swells and peaks, which quickly

grew bigger and bigger.

"Tom." Elenna's voice sounded as if she could hardly speak for fear. "It's a tidal wave!"

RACE AGAINST THE SEA

Tom froze.

"Tom!" Elenna tugged hard at his shoulder.

Wrenching on the reins, he brought Storm's head round and dug his heels hard into the horse's side. "Run!" he yelled.

Storm leapt forward like an arrow from a bow. Yelping fiercely,

Silver raced along not far behind.

"Faster!" Elenna cried. "The wave's catching up."

Tom risked a glance over his shoulder. Now he could see a huge wall of water rolling closer. He couldn't believe how fast it was coming.

He bent low over the horse's neck. "Come on, Storm," he urged. "You can do it!"

The path led back towards the hills. Could they reach the higher ground before the wave crashed down upon them?

Glancing back again, he saw Elenna's face was white with terror. Her hair was whipped back by the speed of their flight. Beyond her the wave reared up, blotting out the sky. The hills where they would be safe seemed very far away.

Then Elenna tugged at Tom's shoulder again. "Over there!" she gasped, pointing to one side.

It was a ridge jutting out into the valley. Smooth slabs of rock, covered in a mossy carpet, stood high above the rest of the land. It might just be high enough for Tom and Elenna to escape the flood.

Tom pulled on Storm's reins and the stallion plunged away from the path. His hooves thundered across the blackened fields.

But the roar of the wave was getting louder. When Tom looked

back, he saw murky green water
rising in a smooth curve behind
him. The top was beginning to curl
over, edged with white foam.

Storm's pace slowed as he started
to climb over the rough ground.
Tom had to cling to the front
of the saddle to keep his seat.
Elenna's arms were so tight round
his waist he could hardly breathe.
He couldn't see Silver, though he
heard the wolf howling.

The slope grew steeper still. Tom
was terrified that Storm would slip
back, into the oncoming wave.

"Faster!" he gasped.

The horse leapt upwards, his
hooves clattering on bare rock as
he fought for balance. Tom let out

a roar of panic. If Storm fell, they would all die!

Then the wave hit the ridge and sea water crashed around them, surging up Storm's legs. Spray shot into the air, drenching them. Tom's eyes stung and he blinked to clear them.

With a last effort, Storm heaved himself onto a spur of rock, while the wave licked hungrily just below. Tom and Elenna slid to the ground.

Storm was sweating and trembling. Tom patted his neck. "Well done, boy. You saved us. You're the bravest—"

"Where's Silver?" Elenna's cry interrupted him.

Tom looked out over the stretch of churning water. Branches and other debris lurched past him. But there was no sign of the wolf.

"Silver! Silver!" Elenna called frantically.

Urgent yapping answered her. Tom spotted a dark shape thrusting through the waves. Silver was paddling furiously towards them. His muzzle vanished under the swirling water, then reappeared. Tom couldn't tell if he was making any headway.

"He can't do it! He'll drown!" Elenna sobbed.

She began tugging off her boots, ready to plunge into the water and grab the wolf.

Tom clutched her arm. "No – it's too dangerous!"

Before Elenna could struggle free, a surge of water tossed Silver closer. His paws thrashed, pushing him up to the rock. With a gasp of relief Elenna knelt on the edge to lean over and grab him by the scruff of his neck, helping him to safety.

Silver was panting hard, and water streamed off his thick coat. "You're safe!" Elenna cried. She threw herself down beside the wolf and hugged him fiercely. "We're all safe!"

"Only for now," Tom said. "I'm sure I saw the sea serpent from the top of the hill. It must have caused the tidal wave. If we don't free it from Malvel's curse, it'll flood the whole kingdom."

Tom touched the sword in his

scabbard. He would free Sepron –
whatever it took!

STRANDED!

Tom pulled the map out of his pocket again. The glowing green path that had led to the shores of the Western Ocean now ended in lapping waves. The tiny figure of Sepron had vanished.

Rolling up the map, Tom looked round. In front of him water stretched as far as he could see. Behind, a rough slope led up to the top of the ridge. A couple of twisted trees stood out against the sky.

"Maybe we can get back into the hills," Elenna suggested. "There must be a way."

Tom pointed to the top of the ridge. "We should be able to see from up there."

With Elenna beside him he climbed the slope. When they reached the thorn trees they stopped in horror.

"No!" Elenna exclaimed.

They were standing on the highest part of the ridge. The lower part, which joined it to the range of hills beyond, had disappeared under the wave. They were now on an island surrounded by a vast lake.

Elenna folded her arms. "Now what do we do?"

Tom gazed towards the west. Out to sea he could see the rocky island jutting from the water. That must be where he had seen Sepron on the map. But without a boat they had no way of getting there.

"What's that?" Elenna pointed to a clump of trees on the opposite side of the ridge.

Behind the trees Tom could make out the grey walls of buildings, and he caught a glimpse of movement. "There's someone there," he said. "Maybe it's a farm."

"Let's go and see," Elenna suggested. "Whoever it is might be able to help us."

"Good idea. But we mustn't say anything about Sepron. The Quest is a secret."

They went back down the slope to collect Silver and Storm. Tom led the tired horse up the ridge and down the slope beyond to the clump of trees on the other side. Elenna followed with Silver at her heels.

As they approached the trees, Tom saw groups of people clustered round a few stone cottages. Lower down the slope, more cottages were partly covered by water. Waves lapped at their windows. Beyond them, Tom could see only thatched roofs, then nothing but unbroken sea.

Elenna's eyes widened with shock.

"It's a village!" she exclaimed. "The water has covered most of it."

"I hope no one was drowned," said Tom, as they approached the water.

At the sound of Tom's voice, a redhaired boy standing at the water's edge turned. "No, everyone's safe, thank goodness," he said.

"We're all lucky to be alive," Elenna said, then added, "I'm Elenna, and this is Tom."

"My name is Calum," said the boy. "Look at this!" He pointed at the flooded cottages. "What are we going to do now?"

"We'll stay and help," Elenna said.

Calum shook his head. "Thanks, but what good can anyone do? We can't live here any more. We'll have to move away, and it's all the fault of the sea serpent."

"The sea serpent?" Tom exclaimed, exchanging a startled glance with Elenna.

A man standing next to Calum said, "You'll think we're talking rubbish. I thought that myself once. But now I've seen the creature. It's

out there. Legend says the serpent
protects Avantia's fishermen and
keeps the sea full of fish, but now it
is doing just the opposite!"

Tom's stomach churned with
excitement. They were in the right
place. With a bit of luck he would
soon be able to face Sepron and
free him.

Calum gestured to the man. "My father and I were out at sea when we saw it," he explained. "It smashed the boat to pieces. I thought we would drown for sure."

"What did you do?" Elenna asked.

"We hung on to scraps of the wreckage and swam ashore," Calum replied. "Every minute I thought the sea serpent would swallow me."

"And that wasn't the first bit of trouble, either," his father added. "For weeks before that, we caught next to no fish. And now we have no boats. A fine lot of fishermen we are without boats!"

"There's one over there." Tom pointed to a small boat lying not far from the edge of the water.

"It's the only one left," said Calum despairingly. "And it's got a hole in it."

"I'll help you mend it if you like," Elenna offered. "My uncle's a fisherman, too, and he taught me how to do repairs."

Calum's father shook his head doubtfully, but a spark of hope appeared in the boy's eyes.

"Let us mend it, Father," Calum said. "At least it's something to do. We shouldn't give up hope yet."

The man nodded slowly. "All right." Then he walked to the water's edge and stood gazing at the sea, as if waiting for the serpent to return.

Tom wished he could reassure the fisherman. As soon as the boat was mended, he and Elenna could row out and find Sepron. But he couldn't tell anyone about his Quest or about the Beast being under an evil spell!

"We need wood for a fire," Elenna said. "And rope and tar to mend the hole."

Calum glanced round. "There's wood and rope scattered all over. And I'll find you some tar." He ran to one of the cottages and vanished inside.

While Elenna started to collect scattered pieces of driftwood, Tom unsaddled Storm and led him to the trees where there was grass for him to eat. He noticed a long branch lying under the trees and dragged it back with him. Then he found some scraps of rope by the water's edge, and began to unravel them.

Calum came back with a burning log from the cottage. A small girl with red hair trotted behind him, holding a pot of tar.

"This is my sister," he said. "She wants to help."

"Hello." Elenna smiled at the little girl and started the fire with the log Calum had brought.

Calum and his sister brought armfuls of bigger branches and laid them on the fire. They crackled in the flames, and smoke billowed into the air.

When Tom had finished unravelling the rope, he and Calum turned the boat over so that they could reach the jagged hole in the side. Tom noticed that the oars were lashed together under the seat. They were lucky. A boat without sail or oars wouldn't be much use.

Tom packed the strands of rope into the hole while Elenna put the pot on the fire and found a stick to stir the tar. When it was bubbling she grabbed the pot handle in a fold of her shirt and carried the pot over to the boat. Quickly she used a scrap of driftwood to plaster the hot tar over the rope strands, inside and out. Everyone gathered round to watch, and Silver whined in approval.

Suddenly Tom heard the fire roaring louder and felt a fierce heat on his back. Silver let out a howl.

Tom turned to see Calum's sister piling more wood onto the fire. The green branches were spitting and crackling as the flames took hold.

"No, stop!" Tom shouted.

The little girl stumbled away from the fire. But it was too late. Flames billowed and the branches hurled out bubbles of hot resin. A spark fell on the pile of branches next to the fire, and more sparks shot into the air. One landed just beside the boat. Calum stamped hard on it to put it out.

But it was no use. The fire was out of control and creeping across the ground towards them!

FIRE AND WATER

Tom looked desperately for his shield. Where had he left it? Then he spotted it at the water's edge where he had put it when he unsaddled Storm. He grabbed it and yelled to the others, "Get away from the fire! I'll make sure it doesn't get to the boat!"

Elenna and the others ran to a safe distance and watched as Tom flung his shield up before the fire, standing as close to it as he dared, with the boat not far behind him. Hot resin spat angrily as flames licked the shield. The heat from the fire singed the hair on Tom's arms, and he could barely hold the shield in place.

"Tom!" Elenna yelled. "It's not safe! Run!"

"No!" Tom shouted. "I'm sure I can hold the fire back!" He turned his face away to protect his eyes from the glare of the angry red flames. His tunic was damp with sweat.

Gradually, the blast of flame grew weaker. Still holding the shield before him, Tom dragged some of

the branches away and the fire
began to die down. Black smoke
curled into the air.

At last Tom lowered the shield. "Is
anyone hurt?" he asked.

Elenna and Calum shook their heads.

The little red-haired girl burst into tears. "I was only trying to help!"

Her father rushed up and hugged her. "It's all right," he said. "There's no harm done." To Tom he said quietly, "It's a good thing the ground was wet from the tidal wave, so the fire couldn't spread too quickly."

Tom looked round. The earth was scorched and steaming. That fire could have spread not only to the boat but to the cottages, and then... It didn't bear thinking about. He glanced over to the clump of trees where Storm was standing – thank goodness the horse had been out of harm's way.

Tom examined his shield and the gleaming bluish-black dragon scale in its scorched surface. Wizard Aduro had been right. Ferno's gift really was a protection against fire!

Looking up, Tom saw Calum and his father staring thoughtfully at the shield, then at him. Tom's stomach lurched. What would he say if they questioned him?

"Let's go back to the cottage," Calum said to his sister, patting her on the shoulder.

Silver raced back along the shore and threw himself at Elenna, who put her arms round the wolf's neck and hugged him.

"Is he all right?" Tom asked.

"Yes, he's fine. He wasn't anywhere near the fire." Scrambling to her feet, Elenna gestured towards Calum's father, who was examining the repair to the boat. "Let's ask if we can borrow the boat."

Tom nodded doubtfully. Would the fisherman be willing to lend them the boat? After all, Tom couldn't tell him the real reason he wanted to borrow it, or how urgent his Quest was. But there was no other way to reach Sepron. And Tom had to save the kingdom!

He walked up to the man. "Sir," he began politely, "may we borrow the boat? We'll take good care of it."

The fisherman straightened up.
"This is the only boat we have left.
Do you think I'm going to give it to
you when we need it ourselves?"

"We'll leave Silver and Storm
here with you," Elenna said, coming
to stand beside Tom. "That way you
can be sure we'll bring the boat
back."

The man shook his head. "I'm not
calling you thieves. But anything
could happen. There could be
another wave, or a storm. And the
sea serpent's still out there. You
might drown, and we'd never see
our boat again."

"But—" Tom protested.

"I'm sorry. The answer's no."

He turned and walked away. Tom

stared after him in frustration. Without a boat, how could they get out to sea and free Sepron?

Elenna spoke close to his ear. "If he won't lend us the boat, we'll just have to borrow it without permission."

Tom stared at her. "What? We can't do that!"

"But we'll bring it back. Tom, you know that there'll be more tidal waves if we don't free Sepron from Malvel's spell. And there'll be no fish in the sea, either. These people will starve. We'll be taking the boat for their own good."

Tom thought carefully. Should he risk offending Calum's family? Or see the whole kingdom destroyed by Malvel's curse? He knew he didn't have a choice.

"We'll take the boat and row out at dawn," he said.

ON WITH
THE QUEST

Tom and Elenna slept on the floor
of one of the cottages. Tom chose
a spot near the door, so he and
Elenna could sneak out without
disturbing anyone.

He woke to feel Elenna shaking
him by the shoulder.

"Come on!" she whispered. "It's
time."

Faint grey light was leaking through the shuttered window into the cottage. Tom rose to his feet, careful not to make a noise, and edged open the door. He and Elenna crept outside.

The sky was growing pale above the trees. Tom could make out the dark shape of Storm, grazing further up the hill. Silver came bounding out of the trees and snuffled at Elenna's hand.

"Sshh, boy," she murmured.

Tom saw that the flood water had almost disappeared during the night. More of the cottages had appeared. The boat was where they had left it, but now it lay at the top of a long slope covered with debris.

"Oh, no!" Elenna's eyes were wide with shock. "How will we get the boat down to the water?"

The boat was small, but it was strongly built. Straining together, Tom and Elenna could barely lift it.

"This is no good," Tom panted, setting it down again. "If we could find some rope we could tie it to Storm and let him drag it."

"No!" Elenna protested. "Look how rocky the slope is. We'd risk smashing another hole in it."

Tom gazed down at the boat. They were so close, but without a boat they would never be able to reach Sepron.

"One more try," he said to Elenna.

"We've got to shift it."

They both stooped down and gripped the upturned boat at the bow and stern. Then a shout came from the cottage they had left.

"Hey! What do you think you're doing?"

Tom let go of the boat and straightened up. Calum was coming out of the cottage. He strode towards Tom and Elenna.

Tom ran to meet him. "Calum, don't wake everyone, please. We can explain."

Calum's face was dark with anger. "I thought you wanted to help us. Now it looks as if you're trying to steal our boat."

"We only want to borrow it,"

Elenna pleaded.

"My father said no!"

Tom hesitated. To his relief, none
of the other villagers had been
disturbed by Calum's shout. If only
he could persuade Calum... But he
knew that he shouldn't tell anyone
about his Beast Quest. That would
only spread panic.

"I need the boat for something
really important," he began.

Calum was giving him a
thoughtful look now. It was the
way he had looked at Tom's shield
after it had turned aside the
flames. Then he glanced out to
sea. "I think I can guess," he said.
"I thought there was something
strange when I saw what you did

with your shield." He paused, then added, "You remind me of someone."

"Who?" Tom asked.

"A man who rode through here a long time ago. He looked just like you."

Tom's heart began to thump painfully. Could it have been his father? "What was his name?" he asked, gripping the boy's shoulders.

Calum shook his head. "He didn't say. He just told us he was on a Quest." He paused then said, "I think you might be on a Quest, too."

Tom was sure that the stranger must have been his father, Taladon. He ached to know more about

him. He wanted to ask about every
detail of his stay in the village,
but there was no time. The sky
was growing brighter – soon the
villagers would be up and about.
And he couldn't tell Calum his
secret, even though he had almost
guessed it for himself. He held the
boy's gaze steadily. Elenna didn't
say a word, though Silver whined
softly.

After a moment, Calum gave a
brisk nod. "All right. I'll help you
move the boat."

The three of them managed to lift
the boat and carry it down the hill.
With the flood water almost gone,
they waded across a pebbly beach
until the sea was deep enough to

launch the boat. Tom and Elenna
scrambled on board. Silver yelped
eagerly and tried to follow.

"No, boy," Elenna said, ruffling
the thick fur round his neck. "You
can't come this time."

"I'll look after him," Calum promised. "And your horse." He rested his hand on Silver's head. The wolf looked up at him and let out a mournful whine.

"We'll be back soon," Tom said.

Tom gave Silver a last pat. Then Elenna unlashed the oars and gave one to Tom. They began rowing out to sea.

Back on the beach, Calum stood knee-deep in water, with Silver at his side. He raised a hand. "Good luck!" he called.

"Thanks," Tom muttered, looking at Elenna. "We're going to need it."

6

DISCOVERY ON THE ISLAND

Rowing was hard work. Sweat plastered Tom's tunic to his body. His hands tingled from gripping the oar. Elenna's hair clung to her face, and she snatched a moment to wipe her forehead.

An eerie silence surrounded them. The only sounds were the creaking of the oars and the slap of

their blades on the water. As they
headed out to sea the water became
choppy. A current seized the boat
and it became harder to row.

Tom's muscles strained as he
thrust the oars deep into the
churning water. They had to keep
going! He squeezed his eyes shut
and tried to ignore the screaming
pain of his muscles. He could hear
Elenna panting with the effort.

Gradually Tom realised that
he could make out the shape of
a rocky island in the misty dawn
light. "Let's head over there,"
he told Elenna. "I think that's
where I saw Sepron, just before
the tidal wave."

He looked over his shoulder,

peering into the mist. There was no sign of the sea serpent. Tom felt an icy shiver down his spine as he thought of the great head rising out of the water.

Then Elenna let out a cry. "Tom! The boat's leaking!"

Tom started. Water was washing round his feet and more was oozing through the repair Elenna had made the day before. He was so wet from launching the boat that he hadn't noticed.

"The tar hasn't had time to set properly," Elenna said. "We'll have to beach the boat and fix it."

"We can't go back to the village!" Tom said, alarmed.

"Give me your oar. I'll row while

you bail. We'll try to land on the rocky island."

Elenna started to row again while Tom cupped his hands and bailed out the water.

The island gradually grew closer, and Tom spotted a narrow strip of pebbles between two spiky crags. "There!" he exclaimed.

The water swirled dangerously round the rocks as Elenna rowed between them, struggling to keep the boat on a steady course. The boat lurched and rocked in the waves. But at last Tom felt the bottom scrape against the pebbles. Puffing out a grateful sigh, Elenna pulled the oars into the boat. Then they both leapt out and dragged

the boat out of the water.

While Elenna packed the rope and tar more firmly into the hole, Tom scooped the rest of the water out of the bottom of the boat. When he had finished, he walked down to the water's edge and scanned the sea. The surface shone silver in the growing light of morning, and was ridged with waves that burst into foam as they hit the rocks.

"Where are you, Sepron?" Tom wondered aloud.

"There!" Elenna said at last. "That should hold it until we get back to shore."

Tom knew that by now the sun must have risen over the hills

inland. But the sea mist seemed suddenly to have grown thicker and he couldn't see the land. The water level had sunk even further. More of the rocks were exposed and seaweed lay everywhere. Tom wrinkled his nose at the smell. A silver fish was flapping helplessly on a flat rock. Elenna gave it a gentle push and it flopped back into the sea.

"What now?" she asked, gazing round.

Tom pulled out the map and hastily unfolded it. "The map shows Sepron in the water beside this island," he muttered. "He must be close." He looked back up at the sea. It was still quiet but

beneath those waves Sepron was
lurking. If that huge serpent burst
through the surface of the water
now, Tom and Elenna wouldn't
stand a chance. There was no point
hanging about. They had to get out
there and find the Beast!

"Let's take a look around,"
Tom suggested. "We might spot
something that will show us where
to find Sepron."
Together he and Elenna
clambered over the rocky base of
the island. There was nothing to

see except more seaweed and tiny scuttling crabs. There had to be a clue somewhere! Then Tom spotted an iron hoop driven into the rock.

"Hey!" he called to Elenna. "Come and look at this."

Elenna hurried over to join him. Examining the hoop, Tom saw that a thick golden chain was fixed to it, leading down into the water. It was draped with seaweed and covered with barnacles, but it still gave off a mysterious glow, which faded as the chain sank deeper into the water.

Elenna caught her breath. "Do you think it's enchanted?"

Tom crouched down and touched the chain, then he nodded. "This

must be what's trapping Sepron!"
he said.

7

SEPRON AT LAST!

"You're right!" said Elenna. "This chain must lead to an enchanted collar like the one on Ferno."

"It's the only clue we have anyway," Tom replied. "We need to follow it. Let's fetch the boat."

Tom and Elenna pushed the boat back into the water. To Tom's relief, the new repair seemed to be holding and the base of the boat stayed dry.

They rowed round the rocks to where the iron ring was holding the chain. Then they pulled the oars into the boat. Tom and Elenna paused to look at each other. It was now or never.

Tom could feel the cold fist of fear in the pit of his stomach. He could see that Elenna felt scared, too. As her hand reached out for the chain, Tom could see it tremble. He put his own hand on top of hers.

"Don't worry," he said. "We'll be all right."

"Will we?" asked Elenna.

Tom tried to smile. Then he shook himself and pulled the chain up firmly.

"Heave!" he said, and the two of

them started to pull on the chain,
which was slippery from the seaweed
that clung to it. Hand over hand,
they followed the chain, as it pulled
the boat out into the sea. The thick
mist folded around them and soon
the rocky island was out of sight. The
surface of the sea was flat now, and
all they could hear was the water
splashing from the chain.

"Try not to rock the boat," Elenna
said.

Tom nodded. It was best not to let
Sepron know they were close until
they were ready. But the chain was
heavy.

"This is hard work!" Tom gasped.

Then the chain slipped through
his hands and fell to the floor of the

boat. The boat lurched and the water grew choppy. Elenna grabbed the side and peered down into the sea.

"There's something there!" she exclaimed. "Something huge."

Tom looked down beside her. Sure enough, a vast, dark shadow was gliding underneath the boat. He froze at the sound of a loud splash.

Something had broken through the surface of the water on the other side of the boat. Huge drops of sea water rained down on him and Elenna.

Tom knew what he was going to see. Bracing himself, he glanced over his shoulder. Elenna screamed.

Rearing out of the sea was the huge head of the sea serpent. They were face to face with Sepron!

The Beast's eyes were huge
and pale, flashing with icy anger.
Shimmering scales covered his head

and neck, and sea water foamed all
around him.

"He's beautiful!" Elenna
whispered.

Tom felt a sudden stab of joy.
For all the Beast's anger, he *was*
beautiful. He should have been
allowed to roam in the sea, instead of
being tethered here by evil magic.

"Look at his collar," Tom said, pointing. "You're right, it's locked just like Ferno's collar was."

A golden chain trailed from the collar down into the sea. Roaring, Sepron lashed his head to and fro, trying to free himself. Then he plunged back under the waves.

The surface of the sea rolled as

he vanished, and the boat rocked dangerously. Tom and Elenna clung to the side until the water grew quiet again.

Tom peered down into the sea. He narrowed his eyes as an idea grew inside him. Sepron was down there, somewhere. But the serpent couldn't hide for ever. Tom knew what he had to do. He had to follow him into its depths.

"I'm going in," Tom said. "If I can hold my breath for long enough, I should be able to unlock the collar with the key Wizard Aduro gave me." He pulled it out of his pocket and held it up.

Elenna gave him an anxious look, but didn't try to stop him. "Be careful," she said quietly.

"Don't worry, I will."

"There must be something I can do to help," Elenna said.

Tom picked up his shield and gave it to her. "Hold this so it reflects the sunlight on the water," he told her. "It'll help me find my way back."

Slipping off his boots and his tunic, Tom sat on the side of the boat. He stared down into the deep blue sea. "While there's blood in my veins," he muttered, "I cannot fail. I will free Sepron!"

He took a huge gulp of air. Then he dived into the water.

8

SEPRON'S KINGDOM

Tom struck out energetically. He was swimming in an eerie, silent world, where everything seemed to move more slowly. The water was dappled by sunlight breaking through from the surface. Silver bubbles of air streamed away from him.

As he plunged deeper the only

sound he heard was the rushing in his ears. The sunlight faded and panic gripped him as he faced the dark depths. He would never be able to hold his breath for long enough. He would drown! He wanted to turn round and swim back to the light.

Then he forced himself to be calm. He couldn't turn back now. This was his Quest. No one else could help the fishermen and free the Kingdom of Avantia from the threat of Sepron. He plunged deeper still with strong, sure strokes.

Then he spotted a shimmering light. It was Sepron's chain!

Tom swam towards it and followed it down. It led between waving fronds of seaweed, which glided gently aside as Tom pushed through them. Shoals of electric-blue fish darted past Tom's face as he pulled himself deeper into the sea. The fish quickly swam out of sight, as if they knew what was about to happen. Further below, coral rose from the sea bed. Lying among the coral was Sepron.

Tom jumped and almost took a huge gulp of water. Sepron's head and the collar with the padlock were closest to him. The sea serpent's enormous body stretched away into the darkness.

As Tom swam closer, the huge head swung round. The Beast's jaws gaped open, revealing vicious rows of teeth. Tom cried out in fear, even though he was underwater, and watched precious bubbles of air float to the surface. Sepron surged up through the water, heading straight for Tom.

Terrified, Tom turned back. Arms and legs pumping, he swam up to the light. The last of his air bubbled away. His lungs were hurting as he fought not to swallow water.

A bright spot on the surface showed Tom where to aim for. He glanced back, sure that Sepron's mighty jaws would snap shut on his legs at any moment. But to his relief he saw the sea monster give up the chase and sink back into the gloomy depths.

A moment later Tom's head and shoulders broke the surface. He trod water, desperately gulping in air. Sunlight dazzled him. When he could see properly he spotted the boat close by, with Elenna still holding up his shield. He had never been so glad to see anything in his life!

"Tom! Are you all right?" she shouted.

"Yes, fine," Tom panted. Though he didn't feel fine. He was exhausted. But he already knew he was going to have to dive down again. He dragged his limbs through the water to Elenna and the boat. Could he really do it once more? "I have to!" he muttered to himself as he swam.

"Did you find Sepron?" Elenna asked.

Tom tried to ignore the bitter pang of disappointment as he admitted that he'd failed. "Found him, but…" Tom was still gasping for air, "…couldn't get close. Got to try again."

"Don't take in too much air," Elenna called. "And try to move slowly so you don't waste it."

Tom nodded, grateful for Elenna's advice.

He trod water until he could

breathe easily again. Then he took
a last gulp of air, but not too much.
Waving to Elenna, he plunged
beneath the surface.

This time he found the chain
more quickly and followed it down
to the coral reef. Sepron was still
lying there, his coils wrapped
loosely about a spire of coral.

Cautiously, Tom swam closer,
keeping behind a wall of rocks
until he could approach Sepron
from behind. He slid through the
water, desperate not to disturb the
serpent. When he was close enough,
he darted forward and grasped the
glowing collar with one hand.

Straight away, the serpent lashed
its head back and forth, trying to
shake him off. Tom clung grimly
to the collar and worked his way
round until he found the lock in the
collar, under Sepron's jutting jaws.

As quickly as he could, Tom took Wizard Aduro's key from his pocket. He thrust it into the lock. But when he tried to turn it, the key stuck. Numb with horror, Tom realised this was a different kind of lock. The key was useless! Sepron's head heaved upwards. Tom lost his grip on the collar and rolled over helplessly in the surging water. One of the serpent's coils grazed his arm and knocked the key out of his hand. It glinted in the glow from the chain and sank towards the ocean floor. Tom watched it despairingly. There was no point in swimming after it. It wouldn't open the lock.

What can I do now? he thought.

How can I free Sepron without a key?

THE LAST CHANCE

Sepron's neck curved round, his hungry jaws reaching for Tom. With failing strength Tom kicked out, driving himself back to the surface. His chest was bursting for air.

Once more he spotted the bright patch of sunlight from the shield Elenna held. Somehow he broke through the surface of the water near the boat, his mouth searching for air. Shaking wet hair out of his eyes, he gasped and panted.

"Tom!" Elenna cried. "Is everything all right? Is Sepron free?"

"No. The key didn't fit." Tom's voice was hoarse. He swam up to the boat and grabbed the side. "And then I dropped it. There's no way to get the collar off."

Elenna's eyes widened in horror. "What are we going to do?"

Tom's eyes fell on his scabbard. "I'll try this!" he said, unsheathing his sword.

Holding the blade out in front of him, Tom plunged down into the sea again. This time he sensed a massive shadow before he reached the bottom, and he realised that Sepron was waiting for him.

The serpent's neck arched over Tom and its sharp teeth closed inches from his foot as he swam deeper. But he couldn't outswim the Beast. He had to unfasten the collar!

His heart thumping, Tom knew he had to act now. His air wouldn't last long, and if he tried to resurface, Sepron would snap him up. *This is my last chance!* he thought.

He turned in the water and drove himself towards Sepron's body. As the huge jaws gaped open Tom swam underneath them and grabbed the collar. Sepron's scaly head lashed to and fro, and Tom could hardly fit the tip of his sword in the lock.

By now he desperately needed air again. His arms and legs felt like lead and the sword was weighing him down as he struggled to turn the blade in the lock. *This has to work!* he told himself. *It has to!* He summoned all his strength, and tried one last time.

The lock sprang open with a mighty judder, throwing Tom backwards in the water. Instantly, Sepron stopped thrashing and the chain began to loosen. Impatient to be free, the serpent snapped at it angrily and tore the golden links apart with his gigantic teeth. The chain and collar glowed a fiery blue for a second, then disappeared. For so long, Sepron had been under Malvel's curse. But now the Beast was free!

10

THE NEXT QUEST

Tom made for the surface, dragging his sword through the water. His head was throbbing with exhaustion and he could hardly move his arms and legs.

Then he felt something nudge him from below. Terror gripped him as he looked down into Sepron's face. But the anger had gone. The serpent's pale eyes shone joyfully.

He gave Tom another nudge, pushing him up towards the light.

As Tom broke the surface, Sepron lifted him right out of the water. Tom clung to the Beast as he stretched his slender neck towards the boat.

"Tom!" Elenna cried out. "The collar's gone. You did it!"

Tom looked up and grinned. "Yes! Sepron is free!"

As the sea serpent lowered his head to set Tom down gently in the boat, something fell from his jaws. Tom picked it up.

"It's a tooth," he said, gazing at the jagged piece of ivory. He looked up at Sepron, but the serpent didn't seem to be in pain. He must have

loosened the tooth when he tore
at the golden chain. Tom reached
up a hand and touched the Beast's
shimmering scales. "Thank you,"
he said. He might have drowned
without Sepron's help.

The Beast dipped his head in
farewell. Then he dived back beneath
the surface. Tom caught a glimpse
of the serpent gliding away into the
open sea. It was beautiful to see

how gently Sepron moved through the waves; he was truly at home. Tom didn't like to think about how cruelly Malvel's spell had changed Sepron into an evil monster. Malvel was hurting the Beasts as well as the Kingdom of Avantia.

"Sepron's free now," he said. "I think we're safe to say that there won't be any more tidal waves. And there will be fish in the ocean once again."

He and Elenna stared at each other for a moment. Then Elenna let out a whoop of triumph. She and Tom flung their arms round each other and hugged in excitement and relief.

Tom started at the sound of a polite cough just behind him. He and

Elenna leapt apart. It was Wizard
Aduro, who seemed to be standing
on the waves close to the boat. But
Tom could see the ocean through
his robe. so he realised that this was
another vision. Aduro was in the city
of Avantia, but he had magically sent
an image of himself so that he could
talk to Tom and Elenna face to face.
It was good to see him.

"Well done!" the wizard said. "I can
see I was right to choose you, Tom.
You've freed Sepron from the evil
spell and made the sea he protects
safe again."

"I couldn't have done it without
Elenna," said Tom.

Wizard Aduro smiled. "You have
both shown great courage," he said.

"All Avantia will be grateful to you. And now," he added, "is that a serpent's tooth that I see there?"

Tom held out the jagged piece. "Sepron dropped it in our boat."

"That tooth is a present from the serpent. Place it in the front of your shield," the wizard instructed him.

Tom picked up his shield. An empty slot glowing with sea-green light had opened up in his shield above Ferno's dragon scale. It shone more brightly as Tom fitted Sepron's tooth into it. Then the sides of the hole closed round the tooth as if the shield had been waiting for it all along.

"Now your shield will protect you from on-rushing water," Wizard

Aduro said. "Not even the fiercest torrent will be able to harm you."

Tom gazed at the shield in wonder. He had already tested it against fire. Now it would protect him from water as well. "Thank you!" he said.

"Don't thank me," said Wizard Aduro, his eyes twinkling. "You won the tooth yourself. With each Beast that you free, your powers will grow."

Tom glanced at Elenna; her eyes were wide with wonder.

"What must we do now?" she asked.

"First, go back to the village," replied the wizard. "Tell your friend Calum that he and his family have nothing to fear now."

Tom nodded. "Yes. And we have to collect Storm and Silver."

"Then you must ride to the mountains in the north," Wizard Aduro continued. "Arcta the Mountain Giant is also under Malvel's curse and is threatening the kingdom."

"What's happening?" Elenna asked.

"Arcta is sending landslides onto the trading town at the foot of the mountains. If the town is destroyed, there will be no trade and the whole kingdom will suffer."

"And it's our job to stop him," Tom said. He could imagine rocks, mud and earth raining down on the town. The people there must be terrified.

"That's right," said Wizard Aduro. "Freeing Arcta is your next Quest."

"I'll do my best," Tom promised.

"The map will help you again," Aduro told him.

"Thank you. I—" Tom began.

But Wizard Aduro's form had started to fade. The ocean shone more brightly through his robes. Then he was gone.

Tom felt a sudden pang of loneliness. He missed his uncle and aunt, and wondered again where his father was. But he had to continue with his Quest. He looked at Elenna. They had faced terrible danger together and survived. He knew they made a great team. Together, they would succeed in the Beast Quest.

"While there's blood in my veins, I'll free every one of the Beasts," he vowed.

CONGRATULATIONS, YOU HAVE COMPLETED THIS QUEST!

At the end of each chapter you were awarded a special gold coin.
The QUEST in this book was worth an amazing 11 coins.

Look at the Beast Quest totem picture inside the back cover of this book to see how far you've come in your journey to become

MASTER OF THE BEASTS.

The more books you read,
the more coins you will collect!

Do you want your own
Beast Quest Totem?

1. Cut out and collect the coin below
2. Go to the Beast Quest website
3. Download and print out your totem
4. Add your coin to the totem

www.beastquest.co.uk/totem

11

Don't miss the next exciting Beast Quest book, ARCTA THE MOUNTAIN GIANT!

Read on for a sneak peek...

CHAPTER ONE

SPRINGING THE TRAP

Tom and Elenna stopped at a fork in the road. The road to the east led towards the farmland of Avantia. The road to the north would guide them into the kingdom's mighty mountains.

Tom knew which one they needed to take to find the next Beast in their Quest. He feared this mission was going to be even more dangerous than the last. Behind him, he felt Elenna shiver as she looked at the mountain peaks in the distance, wrapped in dark, ominous clouds.

"Let's go, Elenna. We'll be all right," Tom said. Then, sensing his friend's nervousness, he added with a smile, "I mean, I've got you and the mutt for protection, haven't I?"

"The mutt? Well, thank you *very* much!" Elenna whistled to her pet wolf, Silver, who was sniffing some bushes nearby. "Come on, boy – let's teach our friend some manners!"

She pointed at Tom, and the wolf bounded across and playfully nipped his heels.

"Ow!" Tom cried.

"Take it back!" Elenna demanded.

"All right! All right! I take it back!" Tom laughed.

Elenna gave another short whistle. Silver immediately left Tom alone and trotted obediently by Storm's side.

Tom smiled. They were in this together.

The four of them set out on the road to the north.

Before he'd met Elenna, Tom had been chosen by King Hugo and his royal adviser, Wizard Aduro, for this Quest. He was to save the Kingdom of Avantia from Beasts who had been trapped by the spell of Malvel the Dark Wizard and were destroying the land. Tom's mission was to free them from the curse, so that they could protect Avantia once more.

He wished with all his heart that his father, Taladon the Swift, could see him as he took part in the biggest adventure of his life. But his father had disappeared when he was a baby.

Before the Quest, Tom thought the Beasts only existed in legend. But now that he had fought and freed two of them himself – Ferno the Fire Dragon and Sepron the Sea Serpent – he knew just how real they were, and how deadly they could be.

So far he and Elenna had survived
by working together. Now they had
to face a new danger that lurked in
the mountains of the north.

Arcta the Mountain Giant.

They travelled north through the
foothills for some time, then Tom
brought Storm to a halt. The trail
before them led up a steep hill,
surrounded by boulders and trees.
"Let's check we're going the right
way," he said. He fumbled for the
magic map Wizard Aduro had given
him and unrolled it. Pine trees and
mountains rose up from the old
parchment, standing as tall as
Tom's thumbnail. The path they

were following glowed.

"Another day's ride and we should reach the town," Elenna said, peering over his shoulder.

Tom looked closely at the map. The town was surrounded by five jagged mountains, and the road leading to it was long and winding. One part looked blocked by a landslide. He touched it and a plume of dust rose up from the map. They might have to find another way round. Tom had never tried to climb a mountain before. Would it be as steep and as dangerous as he imagined?

"We'd better make camp soon," he said. "We're going to need all our energy to get up that mountain pass tomorrow."

They continued up the hill. At the top they stopped suddenly. Mountains stretched as far as they could see. Dark shadows filled the folds and gullies, while the summits seemed to blaze in the late afternoon sun. Like rows of sharp teeth, the mountains stood out against the deep-blue sky.

"It's beautiful," whispered Elenna.

Tom nodded. He'd seen many things on his Quest so far, but no landscape as breathtaking as this.

They noticed a ragged group of men coming down the trail towards them. Tom gripped his sword.

One of the men called out a greeting as they drew near. Tom could see he was carrying a young boy over his shoulder.

When the group reached them, Tom and Elenna saw that the men were traders. But they looked dirty and tired, and the boy appeared to be injured – his head was wrapped in a bloody strip of cloth.

"Can you help us?" the man carrying the boy asked. "Do you have any water? All our supplies have been destroyed."

Tom immediately passed him his water canteen. "What happened?"

"We were part of a trading caravan, bringing supplies to the town," the man explained, setting the boy down and giving him some water. "There was a landslide and we were lucky to survive."

"What triggered it?" asked Elenna.

"We don't know. The mountains are usually very stable. But the weather was odd and—"

"The giant..." spluttered the injured boy. "It was a giant..."

Tom and Elenna exchanged glances.

"Don't mind Jack," one of the men said quietly. "He got a bump on the head."

The first man said grimly, "I hope you two aren't going into the mountains."

"I'm afraid we are," said Tom.

"The mountains are dangerous, even in the best conditions," he warned, looking concerned. "The main road is blocked now and the weather's bad. I'd turn back. That's what we're doing."

"We don't have a choice," Tom said bravely.

Read
ARCTA THE MOUNTAIN GIANT
to find out more!

Discover the new Beast Quest mobile game from

PLAY GAMES

Available free on iOS and Android

Guide Tom on his Quest to free the Good Beasts
of Avantia from Malvel's evil spells.

Battle the Beasts, defeat the minions,
unearth the secrets and collect
rewards as you journey through the
Kingdom of Avantia.

DOWNLOAD THE APP TO BEGIN
THE ADVENTURE NOW!